ONE L

"A Scottish Historical Time Travel Romance"

William Newell

© 2016 SubArctic Publishing

All rights reserved.

~ One Last Time ~

Disclaimer

This is a work of fiction. Names, characters, businesses, places, events and incidents are either the products of the author's imagination or used in a fictitious manner. Any resemblance to actual persons, living or dead, or actual events is purely coincidental.

No part of this publication may be reproduced, distributed, or transmitted in any form or by any means, including photocopying, recording, or other electronic or mechanical methods, without the prior written permission of the publisher, except in the case of brief quotations embodied in critical reviews and certain other noncommercial uses permitted by copyright law.

Stories In This Series:

Book One: Passage Through Time

Book Two: Return to Scotland

Book Three: The Forbidden Rescue

Book Four: Alone in Time

Book Five: One Last Time

Book Six: Into The Rennaisance

Dedication

"To all who long to live the romantic era.
This book was created for you."

CONTENTS

Chapter 1: The Project

Chapter 2: The Fields

Chapter 3: Culloden

Chapter 4: Iona

Chapter 5: Pressed Into Service

Chapter 6: On the March

Chapter 7: The Choice

Chapter 8: The Battle of Culloden

Chapter 9: Last Reunion

Chapter 10: All Good Things

Book Preview

Chapter 1
The Project

Dungallow, Scotland
October 25, 2019

John and Katie Duncan were sharing their quiet Highland Scottish cottage alone together for the first time in a week. They sat on the frumpy, tired-looking couch Katie had picked up in an estate sale, an eyesore that was comfortable enough they'd each lost hours napping in that spot on many quiet, cool afternoons like this one. Outside, the leaves were turning colors in the cozy village of Dungallow. The American-born couple were sipping their tea, emotionally struggling to fend off the growing feeling that their marriage was, once more, on the brink of failure.

"You're sure you don't mind?" Katie asked for the fifth time that day.

John sighed, then laughed to try to break the tension. "No. It's really okay. I'll snap some photos, you'll check out the battleground- we touch nothing. Right? Nothing."

"Absolutely." She nodded her head firmly. She wasn't that absolute about it at all, but she did want to reassure her husband and work to rebuild bridges burned down that summer.

On the surface, the idea seemed a terrible one. As a writer, Katie was used to these sorts of trips, voyages of discovery into her own past. Over the past few years, she'd focused her work on controversial tales of time travel. She and John had gone back to pre-Roman Scotland, the time of the Highland Clearances, and the World War II blitz on Clydebank. Her first book, placed in ancient Caledonia, was told as a true story because, as Katie liked to tell people, it had actually happened to her. General reception had ranged from acceptance to amusement to charges of being a profiteering liar. Regardless of the negative opinions, she felt better in her new, post-journalism career. It had been therapeutic.

Not that they needed the money from her writing. On their return from the 1940's, John and Katie had managed to rewrite history, saving countless Scottish lives and inheriting a surprising fortune. During their celebratory trip around the world, Katie had independently returned to early Medieval Scotland, the time of the Norse raiders. Instead of returning within a short time span, she'd spent years of her life there, building a marriage with the second love she'd come to known. Though she hadn't told John everything about this trip, the natural changes inside her from living years beyond his and the tension upon her return- mere moments in the perception of the modern world- was driving them apart.

They'd seen a marriage counselor. Privately, she was seeing a therapist as well. Though the therapist had openly expressed her skepticism of Katie's story, she'd been helpful.

To be fair, "how do I tell my husband about a marriage from over 1,000 years ago," doesn't lend itself to easy analysis, Katie thought.

"I don't want to be in the way." As John drank his tea, she noted that his hand was shaking slightly. He'd been doing that a lot, of late. She reached out to steady his hand, but he pulled away.

"I only wanted to look at your hand!" She cried out. Realizing she sounded defensive, she softened her tone. "I really wish you'd see a doctor about that.

"It's nothing." He replied, bristling. "Seriously, nothing to be concerned about." He grew quiet, but she couldn't shake the feeling that, like her, he was hiding something from her. Whatever was happening, marriage counseling wasn't helping.

She set down her own drink and snuggled in next to him. "I'm sorry. I don't know... I don't know why we can't just talk. I don't mean to pry."

He nodded. "I guess I'm feeling a little homesick. It's wearing on my nerves." Originally from Chicago, the couple had emigrated after feeling an undeniable, almost instinctual pull to live closer to their roots.

"Do you want to visit Chicago?" She asked, looking up at him.

He shrugged. "Might make it worse to do that. I love Scotland, don't get me wrong. I just want to stay here. Now. I want you here, too." He looked away as he said this, and she felt herself tense up.

"I didn't choose to make the jump, you know." He pulled away from him, standing. "You can stop acting all hurt, as though I wanted to get away or something."

"Maybe you did. Maybe that's why I didn't go with you." He complained.

"This is ridiculous. You know, I just wanted a nice day together for once. Damn it!" She spun on her heel and fled to the upstairs bedroom.

Money, fame, it hadn't mattered after all, she decided, throwing herself on the bed. They still couldn't change themselves, no matter where they went.

***

It only took John ten minutes to realize they'd had an argument over something she couldn't control, like sneezing or hiccups, and he was the bad guy. He felt stupid.

Looking down at his hands, he saw there were small tremors returning. He tried to shut that out of his mind. Hard to hold a camera steady with that going on. He could always go to a tripod on a regular basis, one day, if that's what it really took. Not that he needed to take photos; they were worth millions. It was just something he felt he had to do.

Like apologizing to his wife, he decided, with a rueful smile.

"Honey?" He knocked at the door. Nothing happened, so he opened it a crack. The room was dark and she was curled up, turned away from him. He walked over to her.

"Any room in there for a jackass?" He asked quietly.

She sniffed and, turning her head, showed him a sarcastic half-smile. "Always has been."

They spooned on the thick comforter Katie's sister had bought and shipped for her that past Christmas. With colder weather coming on, it was a nice creature comfort for the room.

"I've decided I don't care about the last jump," he said, referring to their pet name for time travel. "I've decided it's not my business. Sorry if I've been weird about that."

She sighed. "I'm scared."

"What are you afraid of hon? That it's going to happen again?"

"No." She turned onto her back and John could see she'd been crying. "I'm afraid it's not going to happen again. And I don't know what that means or why I feel that way, but I do."

Chapter 2

The Fields

Drummossie Moor, Scotland
October 27, 2019

"Can we stop or not?"

John scrunched up his face in annoyance at the snapping tone of his wife's question. They'd spent much of the morning driving in silence or exchanging curt words as they stared out at the road ahead. It had felt much longer than three hours to John.

"Yeah. Of course. We'll cut into Inverness first…"

"I wanted to stop right away for coffee."

~ One Last Time ~

"It's two minutes away, okay?" He informed her, with a little more force to his voice than he intended.

She shrugged and looked out of the window.

This was a continuation of a fight they'd had the night before. They were no closer to resolving it and he was embarrassed to admit to himself he could no longer even recall what they were arguing about.

When they reached the outskirts of Inverness, they took a sharp turn into a mini-mall and found an open coffee shop. While they were waiting for their beverages, John decided he ought to try to ease things with Katie with the olive branch of light conversation.

"Been awhile since we've done one of these trips." He mused. "You forget how pretty the countryside is."

She said nothing, offering him a slight nod, so he continued. "We should visit a castle on the way back. Of course, we won't touch anything. Wouldn't want to get carried away." He gave her a wink at that and she smiled slightly.

"I wouldn't mind that. Do we have to hurry back? Maybe we could drive along the coast or something." She paused after saying that, and looked away. "You don't have to."

"No, that'd be cool." He actually had plans later that day with friends, but he'd cancel them for a chance to sooth things with her. "Any particular direction? We could go further north to John o' Groats. Or we could head towards Aberdeen and Edinburgh."

She shrugged and retrieved her coffee when offered by the barista.

"Oh, either way. Probably north. But we can figure it out later."

The small token of friendliness seemed to have made a difference. They had another three miles to drive to reach the town of Culloden, and a further three miles south to reach the battle site of Drummossie Moor. All along the way, she was far chattier and he was careful to remain friendly in his responses. It was a small breakthrough in their impasse, but he'd take it.

As they pulled up to the battle site and stepped out, they each shivered a little. It was growing colder, and the chill wasn't helped by a bitter wind blowing across the open moor. They were the first ones at the historic location so they had the place to themselves for the moment.

"So. This is it." Katie said, clearly unimpressed.

He chuckled. "So it is. Look." They stood a short distance from a stone memorial. Just the sight of the imposing figure caused them each to step back. They weren't taking chances; it was always possible that as a relic, they had a history with it.

John grabbed out his tripod and camera from the car while Katie cradled her coffee and scanned the horizon. He hadn't wanted to ask her about the cryptic remark she'd begun and hadn't finished two days ago. She'd mentioned being afraid she'd never make another jump through time- and that had struck him as odd. Why would she fear that?

He hadn't had the heart to ask then, and he wasn't about to wreck her improving mood by asking now. Besides, there might be a reason he didn't want to hear.

Put it out of your mind, he thought. *If you're forgiving whatever happened in her past, you better work on forgetting too. It can't come up all the time.*

"Good thing it's not raining, I guess." She offered. The wind was whipping her long red hair – recently dyed, as it had started to go a touch grey – far behind her. She took a few quick sips to warm herself.

"That could still happen. Wait a minute. It is the Highlands, after all."

"True, I suppose." She admitted. Katie was standing a short distance and was walking towards a small rock she'd spied. When she was in good view of it, she stepped quickly away.

"What is it?" He asked. She looked frightened.

"Nothing. I- sorry, nothing really. It's a little memorial. I didn't want to risk it."

"I understand. We should be okay. There's just a few things here to touch and we're not going to do that, are we?" Another car was approaching.

"No, we are not." She agreed emphatically. She looked over the fields again, biting her lip.

John had set up his shots and was taking them. He smiled to himself; his hands were rather steady today. Whatever was making them shake wasn't as bad, and that was a relief. He'd done a couple of Web searches on the symptoms already. What he'd found wasn't good, so he resisted doing further investigation in the hope that it would simply go away.

Perhaps it was doing just that, he thought, and caught a nice picture of the larger memorial structure moments before the other visitors wandered over to it.

He looked up from his photos and saw Katie was looking glum again. "Something on your mind?" John asked, wishing there wasn't.

"1500 Jacobites, 50 British soldiers... or maybe 300, I guess, according to some sources. A lot of dead. It's bringing back memories." The first time they'd been pulled into the distant past, John had been speared in the foot and Katie had ended up rescuing him.

"Long time ago, dear. Long for us and for real." She reminded him. They'd been fighting the Romans, it had turned out, and had stepped into the lives of ancient Caledonians. He had eventually recovered, but it wasn't an experience he ever hoped to relive.

"Need to frame up this next shot. Wait there, okay?" She agreed silently, drinking her coffee.

He strolled further into the moor, though being careful to be respectful and not go too deep in. As he set down his tripod, his foot struck something hard and sharp.

"What the hell?" He muttered and reached down to pull whatever it was out of his shoe. It appeared to be a very small piece of sharp old, rusted metal.

"Stupid leaving something like this here." He said to himself and dropped it into his pocket without thinking about it. A moment later the thought strayed into his mind that it might not be a modern item at all. His skin grew clammy with fear as he pulled it out of his pocket again to look.

Long and sharp, he thought. Like the tip of something. "A pitchfork?" He said out loud, wondering how a farm implement's remains would have found itself there.

He quickly dropped it, but just as quickly gave a mighty yawn. A veil of heaviness dropped across his eyelids. John was getting sleepy, as sleepy as the times they'd traveled through time.

It was too late to do anything about it. He turned to Katie, who happened to be gazing in the opposite direction towards the woods. "Hon..." He tried to shout, but his own voice sounded distant. She heard him though, and he barely caught sight of her panicked face as he fell face forward, tumbling into the past once more.

~ One Last Time ~

Chapter 3
Culloden

Drummossie Moor, Scotland

October 27, 1745

John felt cool grass against his face. It was neither surprising nor welcome.

When he looked up, the moor and the forest looked much as it had before he'd lost consciousness. There were a few notable differences. The most obvious was the missing stone battle monument. As that registered in his mind, he looked about and realized that their cars and, indeed, the car park were entirely missing from the scene.

John groaned and rolled over. They'd been shot back in time to- when? The actual time of the battle? It couldn't be precise; there were no sounds of war.

"Katie? Do you see anyone else?" He shouted out. "I'm really sorry. I guess I accidentally... Katie?"

He sat up as a horrible thought raced through his mind. He'd expected her to be nearby. She wasn't.

In fact, he was entirely alone.

John stood and glanced at his clothing. A quick guess and, judging by the simplicity of the attire, he was in an era in which peasants were common. Whatever century it was, his clothes were brown, worn, and boring. But he had an uneasy idea of what time he'd arrived in.

Alone without any reference, he decided to try to head in the rough direction he recalled driving in from. There was no road though... not anymore, or probably more accurately, not yet.

It wasn't a good feeling to have time travelled, but given that this was his fourth such trip, he wasn't particularly panicked. Mostly concerned. It wasn't impossible that Katie had made the jump and he just didn't know it yet. They'd arrived separately twice before and found one another. So it seemed at least possible she was somewhere else.

But somehow, he doubted it. This time he suspected he was on his own, as she had been in the last time jump.

Looking down at his hands, he found they belonged to a young man's, probably someone in their twenties. That was fine; he didn't mind jumping into a younger body than his own. It meant he'd have more energy for whatever adventures lay ahead.

It was a very long, cold walk as it turned out. Whatever time of year it was, Spring or Fall, he hadn't evaded the cold. He stalked along the woods, wilder than he recalled it to have been, keeping the moor to his left. He was lost in his own thoughts for more than two miles when a yell brought him out of his reverie.

"Stand!" A deep, booming voice called out from the woods. Its owner had a thick Scottish brogue, the sort that usually threw John for a loop and made it impossible to understand what was being said. But he grasped the idea of the words, regardless. "Give up your valuables,

John of Culloden, lest I run ye through with this blade!"

Someone knew his name and seemed to think he was rich. He checked again; there was no pouch, nothing on him where he might carry money.

"I've nothing, sir. I am but a poor man. Please let me pass unharmed."

Three men stepped out of the thicket, one old gray beard holding a bow and aiming an arrow at John's chest. The thinnest had his arms crossed and cast a menacing glare at him, but he wore a short blade at his hip. It was the third brute, huge in dimensions and weight, which set him on edge. The sandy-haired man lumbered towards him.

"Poor are ye? Well, we'll just double-check, to satisfy our own curiosity."

The fellow quickly closed the distance between them with his great hairy arms outstretched. John surprised himself by dropping low, ducking under the man's reach, and quickly putting him in a headlock. He allowed the hulking man to fall backwards on him, in part to block the man with the bow and to help himself finish the choke.

"Enough! Enough, damn you John!" The man shouted, and he heard the other two attackers cackling. The old man set his bow down and the two approached casually, as two old friends would a comrade.

Their entire demeanor had changed and their manner, for some reason, put John at ease. He found himself smiling and, after a moment's consideration, let his attacker go. He was relieved when the big man stood and reached down to help him up.

"How many times have I told you to venture into these wild lands with only Andrew, Malcolm or myself?" The old man said after clapping him on the back. "There's as likely to be cutpurses as your brothers and I, you know."

"Ah, now pa, John held himself up well enough I should say." The thinner man suggested. He looked John over, appraising the man. "You've gotten nimble brother. Not so nimble as to best me, naturally."

Seeing another friendly attack was imminent, John fell into a fighting stance, but the older man stepped between them. "Now, enough of that, enough of that! You two can have it out on time that's not my own. There's work to be done back in town, you know."

The two younger men grumbled, but kept their complaints low and polite. As he watched them step back into the woods, John quickly followed behind them. He had no idea where he was going, but he presumed his family knew.

Under the canopy of the cool, shady forest, the four men chatted back and forth about the work that awaited them in the village. To his disappointment and surprise, he realized his larger brother Malcolm, his elder, thinner brother Andrew, his father, and he were all blacksmiths. It was work he'd done before during the Clearances, so he sighed and shook his head.

History repeated itself, it seemed.

Chapter 4

Iona

Glasgow, Scotland
November 5, 1745

On the streets of Glasgow, John was surprised to find Katie and even more surprised when she was nearly run down and killed right before him.

He, Andrew, and Malcolm had gone to Glasgow at his father's suggestion to look for work. There was only enough work for two of the Duncan's to continue on with what they were doing, so it made sense for them to travel together and elsewhere; whichever of them couldn't find work would come home and continue in the trade with their father. The young men had an uncle in Glasgow and he was dubious about the three boys staying with him for a protracted length of time, even if they were paying for their own food.

After a breakfast of porridge, the three had wished each other well and parted ways. John had reached a busy street and was fascinated by the speed with which one of the heavy carriages was barreling down the street when he spied a young woman frozen with a look of terror on her face.

He recognized that long red hair anywhere. It was his Katie.

John dashed into the street and slammed into her with his shoulder, shoving her out of the carriage's path. A horse's flank butted into his other shoulder, whirling him along the cobble and muck street and into the gutter beside his wife.

He stood quickly and reached down with a hand to help her up. Though he offered the woman a friendly smile, he was surprised to see the returned look was one of pure fury.

"You country simpleton!" She shouted, refusing his help and gathering up her skirts as she found her footing. "Has no one told you how to treat a woman, and one who is a stranger to you at that? How dare you throw me to the street so rudely!"

"What?" He was genuinely confused. "But the carriage..."

"Yes, I did take note of it! I was turning my mind to escape when you did rush out, unasked, and have now ruined my frock." She looked down at the ruined clothing in despair. "I'd just bought it as well. Catastrophe!"

He was lost without words. She considered him one last time, shook her head in anger and turned to leave.

"Wait! Katie, don't go!"

The woman didn't even turn her head, so John reached out and grasped her arm. She shook it loose.

"Sir, I don't know who you think I am, but that is not my name!" She insisted. "Lay hands upon me again, and I will… well, I don't know! Call for help, I should say."

He backed away, as the people in the street who had initially applauded his efforts were now eyeing him suspiciously. He thought quickly. "Forgive me. I mistook you for a lady of gentle bearing I know. You have her qualities, you see. I apologize most humbly."

She started away, but paused and this time did look back. "You say I am like another? How like her am I?"

"My lady, you could be twins, truly. I would not so have imposed on you so on the street as I did had I known you were not she. May I at least escort you home?"

"I know the way." She laughed. Her dark mood had lifted and she now seemed to think the whole thing something of a joke. "Well, now I have been rude. You intended no harm at all. Yes, I will allow it."

"I am most grateful, ma'am."

"Speak no more of it."

They continued along the walk, she, trying to brush away the dirt and grime from herself and he, keeping a respectful distance between her and the road. "If you are not my friend, may I ask your name?"

She gave him a half-smile. "Iona Buchanan. And you are?"

"John Duncan of Culloden. It's a far distance from here."

"I wonder that you should have a friend in this town, sir, if you are from so far afield."

"I..." He tried to think of an excuse and finding none, went with the truth. "I did not expect to see her here. It now makes some sense as to why you are not she, but the similarity was quite striking." The closer he looked at her, the more he realized Iona wasn't his Katie. When he and his wife had travelled in the past together, they'd looked precisely the same to one another, regardless of whose lives they were inhabiting. This woman's nose was a little smaller, her lips a bit fuller, her eyes not quite as bright. She was beautiful and reminded him of his love- but it wasn't her.

"She must have a strong hold on your heart to inspire such bravery, sir. You really must forgive my reaction. I see now you were attempting gallantry, though I fear it wasn't necessary."

"I apologize again, ma'am."

"As I said before, let's speak no more of it. What brings you to Galway, if not to find this woman?"

He explained his situation and that of his brothers'. "I fear I cannot help your kin, but be of good cheer. Hope lies but a little ways ahead."

She pointed just up the street and he saw a sign with the face of a boar on it. "Let's meet my father, the proprietor." She suggested, brightening. "And let no good deed go unrewarded."

Chapter 5

Pressed Into Service

Glasgow, Scotland
December 24, 1745

The Boar's Head Tavern and Inn was surprisingly busy on the wintery evening John and Malcolm trudged back to their workplace and home. John had grown comfortable with his job as cook, stable boy, and bouncer. He was helped in part by his brother Malcolm handling the bulk of the crowd control while he did most of the cooking; it was better that way. They shared work in the stables as much as it was needed.

Despite Iona's assurance that there was work only for him, he was relieved when her father, one-eyed Donald Buchanan, had pumped his hand enthusiastically and thanked him profusely for saving his daughter's life. "Sure there's work for you and your kin, sure enough. Stable boy has run off with a girl and truth be told a rougher crowd is chasing off much of our more regular visitors. It's grown so that I feel unsafe with my own daughter serving drinks, I am."

"A bit of freshness and a thrown chair now and again we don't mind, you see." Iona had told John by way of explanation. "But there's been more raised ire of late because… well, I think you can guess why."

Earlier in the week, he'd made sure of the date by careful conversation. He had no doubt of why things were so tense. With "Bonnie Prince Charlie," also known as Charles Edward

Stuart, on the march in England, emotions were running high in cosmopolitan Glasgow. Those who didn't share the same faith were quick to raise voices, fists, and at times even blades to settle their scores. However, with Christmas Eve upon them he hoped that people would be a little less likely to attempt to do harm to one another. Not that the holiday was a big deal in this time period, he knew, but it was still to be hoped that the tensions of the Jacobite Rising could be set aside for the holiday.

He knew that eventually Charlie would head north, but for the life of him he couldn't remember the exact date. Wasn't it in the Spring of next year? The Jacobites would eventually wind up where John had awoken and there they would meet their defeat at the hands of the English Duke of Cumberland.

But all of that was a long ways off. For the moment, he and Malcolm were trudging through the snow and rubbing their hands for warmth.

"You think these are enough potatoes?" He asked his brother. They'd had to go out for a food run. Most days they would spend in the inn or tavern doing odd jobs. If there was truly nothing better to do, they could relax in the small space where they made their home above the stables.

Malcolm shifted two massive burlap sacks that were slung over each shoulder. For his part, John could manage one and a smaller sack of onions. "I suppose this'll do for some time. It'll have to! Hearin' rumors of war."

John scoffed. "War's to the south, brother."

"Aye, but coming this way." The big man countered. "I heard Davy MacDonald say as much last night. Well in his cups he was, but he was sure Charlie is coming here, and soon. Such talk will surely make the price of everything dear."

"That it will." John mused. If that were true, it seemed that his timeframes for when things were happening were slightly off. If Stuart were coming back to Scotland now, how soon would it be before he was bound further north to his doom?

They were soon back to the tavern as the light was failing. Iona stepped out just long enough to greet them breathlessly. "Hurry along, lads! More customers by the hour, it seems, and we can't keep them fed or drunk enough!" Her eye lingered on John a moment before she rushed back into the tavern.

Malcolm chuckled. "How much longer you plan to keep that one chasing after him."

John elbowed him in the ribs. "Leave my business to myself and make your business your own."

"Seems there's no business going on with you! For my part, I plan to bed the Irish fishmonger's daughter soon. Just you watch."

"Watch? No thanks!" Malcolm tried to hit him with a sack of potatoes, but John ducked once again and rushed into the tavern.

They were well into their cooking and arguing about women, war, and fighting tactics as they so often did when a cry went up within the bar.

The brothers exchanged a worried glance at the tone of the alarm and ran out of the kitchen and in among the patrons.

Davy MacDonald, already very drunk at this early hour, nearly ran into them. "They've taken her!"

"Who? Who's taken who?" John grabbed the little man and stopped him from running off with his mug of beer.

"Jacobites! They came in and were very rude. Your Iona had words with one and he and his lads grabbed her up quick as you like and were off with her. We tried to stop them, but they was armed, you see…"

He didn't wait to hear more. Malcolm was only a few steps behind John as they rushed out into Galway's dark streets. They heard shouting in a nearby alley and made for it.

Once in the darkened alley, John looked about, trying to get his eyes to adjust. "Do you see anything brother?"

"No one." Malcolm said, just before giving a startled cry. John tried to turn his head, but he felt something heavy slam into the back of his head. The world fell away at his feet.

Chapter 6

On the March

Dungallow, Scotland

December 30, 1745

John and Malcolm found themselves deep in the Highlands when John gave his brother a wry smile.

"I know this place." He said, as Stuart's army marched closer towards the small hamlet.

Malcolm had been staring at the ground during the long northern trek of the past few days. They'd spent a day or two in Galway, always under the watchful eyes of the press gang that had forced them into service. There would be no returning to the Boar's Head for either of them.

Or for Iona.

"That's impossible." Malcolm replied with obvious annoyance. "You've never been anywhere that I know of but Inverness and Culloden. How would you know this?"

"It's Dungallow. Trust me- I know it."

They said nothing more, lest their closest officer in the regiment shouted them down. They carried food and bedding in a rough sack slung over their shoulders and each had been outfitted with a joke of a weapon; a dull knife for Malcolm and a pitchfork for John. He thought he recognized it from the Boar's Head stable, suggesting to him it had been requisitioned. Glasgow was fortunate not to have been sacked entirely; Stuart had threatened to do as much if the inhabitants hadn't agreed to be generous in provisioning his forces.

"I'm going to check on Iona." John notified his brother.

The big man nodded. "Have a care you not be discovered."

John slowed his march just enough to fall back to the horse-drawn cart where they were carrying the young woman amidst food supplies. She had been abducted as a means of drawing the brothers out and waylaying them. Unfortunately, in the process she'd fought one of the men and been wounded for her efforts. A large, ugly gash across her back had become a grievous wound and she'd been knocked unconscious as well, staying under much longer than the Duncan brothers. The men had abducted her anyway, but when their officer found out days later, he'd been incensed. It was too late to return to Galway and safety, so he had put the company's physician to work on healing her injuries.

John spotted the young, dark-haired man by the name of Graham. Graham was desperately trying to defog his glasses, a nearly pointless effort in the chill weather.

"How is she doing, Doc?" John asked. The young man, usually of an extremely morose disposition, grinned as he asked his question.

"Ask her yourself! She's well enough to speak, aye ma'am?"

Iona was riding along in a small supply cart next to the two men. At the sound of John's voice, she tried to sit up, but Graham pressed her back down. "Talk. But rest. You'll need it."

"I'm fine. Really, doctor, I don't need these ministrations." She coughed and tried to smile. "All right, I'll allow as that I need perhaps some. My head aches greatly still."

John looked her over. The red-haired woman was paler than she'd been before and she was sweating. Though she was bandaged and awake, the fever wasn't a good sign and John knew it. He looked Graham in the eye again, as he had the first time he'd met him a few days prior.

"You are definitely washing your hands as I said? Using soap and making sure her bandages are clean?"

The man was slightly annoyed, but equally amused as he'd been the first time John had approached him. "Where a simple country fellow would know such things is beyond me, but aye. I take all of the proper precautions. I'm not without some learning, my friend." Graham gently reminded him with a snicker.

Though he knew he'd be missed in his position further up, John lingered, gazing at Iona. The similarity with Katie caused him an unavoidable attraction; one he regretted but felt he couldn't do anything about. It was maddening; he wanted to reach out and take her hand, tell her she'd be okay. But propriety and the fact of his real wife back home kept him at bay.

He caught her looking back at him. Their eyes met briefly and he forced himself to avert his eyes.

"Well, please let me know how she feels." He stiffly told Graham. "And keep the men away from her. Let me know if any of them try anything untoward."

"Oh, most certainly Captain John." The doctor joked, but he ignored it and sauntered back to his place.

As the army arrived at Dungallow, several locals on the street ran back into their homes, shuttering their windows and praying they wouldn't be bothered. Their efforts to avoid being harassed came to nothing. John soon found himself under orders and forced to pound on a door. He was glad he and Malcolm had been partnered for this task; he knew they'd be honorable together, unlike some of the others in the company.

An elderly woman reluctantly let them into her destitute home. A few children and a hungry-looking mother were seated next to the fire. As they looked about at the hovel, John motioned for Malcolm to watch the door.

"Don't worry, ma'am. We'll take nothing." John said. He reached into his bag and brought out a few tidbits of his last portion of food: bread, cheese and a potato. He smiled and held out the large potato.

"It's not much, but it'll serve for your dinner, don't you think?"

The old woman smiled, gratefully taking the offered food. "Linger a touch longer, good Christian soldier. I'll make us a stew. We've a little more I can spare for the benefit of us all."

He shook his head. "We'll be moving on shortly. But we'll both stay here a bit longer to make sure no one troubles you."

"Bless you both." She said. John looked out of the window and saw Iona's cart passing by. She was sitting up and smiling at him when their eyes met.

~ One Last Time ~

Chapter 7

The Choice

Dungallow, Scotland

April 2, 1746

"I find it a strange world indeed, Miss Iona, that you should now be attending me." Doctor Graham Kinnaird coughed as he lay on a cot that had been set up in the makeshift field hospital. Iona was busily replacing the wrap around the man's shattered right arm and snuck a glance at John. The look on her face told him everything he needed to know; Graham was dying. But for now, she was keeping up a brave face.

~ One Last Time ~

"Now, Doc, let me be your physician as you so thoughtfully nursed me back to health these many months." She quietly reminded him. "It is merely a kindness repaid."

"Aye, but you cannot hide from me the nature of my wounds. The arm is ruined. My belly has too much lead in it. The enemy has won the battle against me. John, I hope it goes better for you. I expect it shall."

John was laying in a cot as well, though his wound was fairly minor. He'd been shot in the foot, but apart from the loss of his little toe, he was expected to be well enough for the next march. Judging from the way the siege of Fort William was going, it would be a forced march, and soon. The pro-government clans weren't weakening at all, thanks to naval support, and only days ago they'd managed to sally out and take most of the Jacobite guns. It was time to move on, and everyone knew it.

It was the second time he'd been wounded during time travel, both times in the foot. Same foot, in fact, John thought with cynical amusement.

But as the good doctor lay dying and coughing on the cot beside them, it was obvious to Iona and John that he wouldn't be going far. He was unlikely to survive their retreat even in a cart, and leaving him to the enemy clan would be cruel. He'd have to take his chances on the road.

Malcolm ventured in soon to confirm their suspicions, after checking up on his brother's health. "We're receiving the orders now. Everything is to be cleared away tomorrow. We go north."

"North to where, I wonder?" Iona mused. John knew, but didn't want to tell either of them. The situation was grim enough. He wondered how he could rescue them, and himself included, from what lay ahead. There was, after all, a likely reason he was here at this point in history. What was to be changed- were they to win the battle? It seemed an unlikely outcome, even more so given he was a simple blacksmith armed with a pitchfork and a missing toe.

"If we go anywhere near our home, we'll rally our kin to us." Malcolm proclaimed, some hope returning to his face. "There's little doubt the Duncan's and the people of Inverness will rise up to fight for Bonnie Prince Charlie!" Shanghaied or not, Malcolm had become a true believer in the cause. As a modern man with no real stake in the battle's outcome, John was indifferent to Stuart's cause. He knew the outcome and, though it was sad, eventually Scotland and England would see an end to the nationalist and religious wars. He just wanted to live long enough to see it.

More than that, he wanted to be back in his little cottage with Katie at his side. There was so much he wanted to say, so much to work out. He'd re-double his efforts at repairing the marriage whenever he got home- soon, hopefully.

It didn't help to put Iona, the woman with Katie's face, out of his mind when she was near him so much these days. She came over to his cot and knelt down beside him.

"You'll be marching again tomorrow. As much as I'd like to keep you off your feet, let's go for a very short walk to test out your footing."

He'd been trying to stand the past few days and it seemed like he should be okay, though it would be a bit painful to march for long miles. He nodded and got up after shaking hands with his brother and bidding him well.

Iona and John stepped slowly through the camp, John leaning somewhat gingerly on the pitchfork and Iona on a pair of crutches. "This will take forever. They'll just leave me behind!"

"We'll see to it you ride in the cart. They'll make you stand and fight, no doubt, but for the time being I think they'll listen to me if I suggest this course of action." Iona had become respected by the physicians and nurses since she'd begun to volunteer, so John didn't doubt her word.

"Listen- Iona. I have something I want to say."

"I had so hoped. Go ahead." Iona was beaming and suddenly John's heart fell.

He'd wanted to find a way to warn the woman about the battle to come, but didn't know how. He thought perhaps a signal would be the thing to do.

But as he found himself growing more comfortable in her presence and more attracted to her, he was torn. What if he could never go home? He knew that Katie had spent years in her own time on the last journey back; so many that she must surely have built a life for herself. Pushing Iona away would mean that if he was trapped here for a lifetime, he might be locking himself off from happiness over his own long years.

He thought about it hard and came to a decision. After squeezing her hand reassuringly, he cleared his throat.

"The battle may go badly against us in the near future. Let me tell you what I propose in order that you survive. Leave early."

Chapter 8

The Battle of Culloden

Inverness, Scotland

Early April, 1746

Iona and Malcolm were helping John as needed as they crested the top of a hill and saw what John had long dreaded.

"That's Inverness, lads!" The officer cried out, and they gave a weary cheer. It was all for show; the thousands were tired, injured, and demoralized. The Jacobites hadn't won a battle since Falkirk, back in January. All most of them wanted was a soft bed and hot food. No one expected to receive either in this far northern town.

Malcolm's joy was genuine, though. John wished he could feel the same. In theory, he was from the place and had cause for excitement. But neither of his companions could understand that.

Swept up in the moment, Iona leaned over and kissed him on the cheek. She was surprised when he drew back and, as he could plainly see, hurt.

When the regiment was settled into Inverness, he waited until they were alone. "Iona, please don't hate me. I can't love another."

She nodded. "It's the one I look like. She must be here, then?"

"I don't know." He answered truthfully.

The woman pet his cheek and stood on tiptoe to kiss his forehead. This time he didn't flinch.

"I wish you much love. I've overstayed my welcome. I'll try to return to Glasgow as soon as I may. But do visit the Boar's Head if you ever return. I'll be happy to hear of your adventures, sweet lad."

He struggled to find the words to express his gratitude appropriate to the situation, but she left him before he could. He would never see her again.

***

"Well brothers. We have gotten ourselves into a fine mess here." Malcolm suggested as a sheet of winter rain fell on them. At his suggestion, they'd gotten word to their brother, Andrew in Culloden of the impending battle. He'd joined them with his sword at the ready, the three men in their plaids and ready for Cumberland's men.

Desperately, John had tried to convince anyone who would listen that the moor of Drummossie, situated as it was so close to Culloden was a disastrous choice for a battleground. The terrain would play directly into the strategies and strengths of their experienced enemies. Unfortunately, the officers seemed to already know this. The decision had been made by Charles Stuart, and no one could shake his decision to lead the charge on this moor.

The three brothers looked out and saw a sea of redcoats awaiting them. "Glad to be at your side, lads." Andrew murmured. "Though,

I'll confess I'd rather we were fighting against a few less of the lobsterbacks"

John glanced nervously at the pitchfork in his hands. He was prepared to march forward, as he'd practiced, though it might be at a slower pace than his comrades. But it was unlikely he'd be able to run well. If desperation called for it, he might. There was Malcolm and Andrew to think of, though, so he tried to put such thoughts aside.

"Here it is then. We go to face them at last." Malcolm said, pulling out his knife.

The order was given. Charge.

They began to run across the moor, using the infamous Highland charge that would settle the Battle of Culloden. Soon, the quiet countryside was filled with the sound of deadly musket fire. John hobbled along as fast as he was able and his brothers kept pace with them. Their tardiness likely saved them from the first assault. Many in the frontline fell, bodies numbering in the hundreds, it seemed. A man nearby clutched at his face and toppled over. Another fell to a knee, then lay prone, his face a mask of horror. But far ahead, hardly any of the English had been harmed.

"Would we had proper guns!" Andrew shouted out. They cast about their eyes for a fallen weapon. Each time they spotted one, a neighbor had snatched it up first.

They were closing the distance too fast, it felt like, and another crack of muskets firing felled hundreds more of the Scots. Despite their efforts, Malcolm, Andrew, and John were now clearly in the rear of the battle.

But there was plenty of battle to go around, so they hurried on.

The trio saw swampy terrain to their left and pushed further to the right to avoid it. As they did so, they encountered the first of the serious close-quarters fighting. Malcolm managed to secure a fallen gun and powder. "Now we're getting somewhere!" He called out.

John grimly hobbled forward, closing in on a British soldier. But as he approached, he heard a horrifying cry from nearby. He looked over in time to see Andrew running to Malcolm's side. The big man was laying on his back.

Forgetting his own attack and the pain from his missing toe, John ran over to where his brother lay. Malcolm had been felled by a single shot to the forehead. Andrew was weeping over the body.

John couldn't help but shed tears as well. They'd grown close in their travels across Scotland. He quickly snatched up the dropped rifle.

"Get out of here, brother." He shouted to Andrew.

"No! We must avenge him!"

"Do as I say. One of us must live. The family will never forgive us if all three of us die here this day."

Andrew considered this and, grabbing Malcolm up under his armpits, began to pull his fallen brother away from the battle.

John turned to face whatever attack awaited him. Instead, he saw two Redcoats facing him, one with a drawn sword and the second quickly loading his musket.

John didn't wait. He took his own unloaded gun and flung it at the man loading his gun. The pitchfork was nearby, so he reached down to get it.

The swordsman was too quick. He stabbed at the place where the pitchfork lay, dissuading him from grabbing it up. Just as quickly as he'd done that, the Englishman swung the pommel of the sword up and connected with John's head.

He felt light-headed as he fell. There was no time to register what would happen next. Instead, he simply stopped thinking altogether.

~ One Last Time ~

Chapter 9

Last Reunion

Culloden, Scotland
October 25, 2019

John opened his eyes, took a deep breath, and sighed. Never a religious man, John took the opportunity to say a silent "thank you" to whatever powers had brought him home. He was equally relieved to realize that his foot was unwounded.

He stood up from the ground where he'd fallen and let the little piece of pitchfork fall back to the ground. He'd lived.

Katie ran over to him, the look of worry on her face blazingly apparent. "You jumped. You went somewhere, didn't you? Did you go…"

"Back to Culloden, yes. I was there. I'll tell you all about it, and I want you to tell me all about your journey. Hold nothing back this time."

They fell into each other's arms, their eyes filling with tears of joy.

John looked over her shoulder at the cold moor one last time at the place where his brother had died. Giving a silent nod, he said farewell.

***

There weren't many words exchanged on the long drive home, but those that were shared were meaningful. John told her everything that had happened in his past. After they had arrived at home and John was unlocking the door, Katie pointed at his hands. "Look. They've stopped shaking."

He glanced down. To his amazement, the persistent tremor was silent. There was no way of knowing if the time travel had impacted whatever had been going on with him. But he breathed a grateful sigh.

"Go and have it looked at anyway."

"I promise I will. This week."

Relieved to be home, they went upstairs. Katie dropped onto the bed, draping an arm over her forehead. "God, in all the excitement I forgot we were going to stay away from home for a while. Remember? We were going to go for a drive and see castles?"

John fell in beside her, running his fingers across her stomach. "Ah, that. Sorry. I really missed home, though. You understand?"

"I definitely do." She turned on her side and held his gaze. "I understand you had your friend- Iona. You were gone a long time. If something happened... I'd understand. You should tell me."

He shook his head. "No, hon. I wasn't there for years as you were on your trip, and besides, she looked far too much like you, yet not. She may have been a relative. Even if she wasn't, that would be strange. I'm married to you, remember? I'm not going to throw you over after just a couple of months away. Your years, though, I mean... if you restarted your life with someone else that was fine."

She smiled. "We'll talk about all of that another time. Just keep rubbing my stomach."

He did as she suggested, slowly working his hand across her belly and along the tops of her legs. Her eyes closed and her lips parted slightly with a little sigh. He leaned over and they met in deep kiss.

John moved his mouth to kiss her cheek, her ear, her neck. They moved in closer on the bed and her own hands were on his back and shoulders. After some time, they began to peel off a piece of clothing at a time for one another, first a shirt, then socks, pants, until their bare skin was touching from chest to entwined feet.

He was kissing her breasts lightly, working from the nipples to the sides of each. Katie reached down and stroked his shaft, feeling him harden in her hand. As they played with each other, John felt inspiration and started to kiss down her stomach.

"What are you doing?" She asked.

"You'll see." He quietly warned, a wicked grin on his face.

By the time his lips met her sex, she was eager for him inside her. "You don't have to." She murmured. But his tasting changed her mind and she arched her back as he pleasured her. John took his time, but wouldn't take things too far. When she could stand it no more, she pushed him away.

"I want it." She demanded with a wry smile. He grinned back and was on top of her, slowly entering and teasing her with light friction and shallow thrusts.

They moved with greater urgency, his hands bracing against the headboard, hers guiding his penetration deeper into her. From time to time, their eyes would lock and they'd feel a strong connection. As their enjoyment mounted they forgot everything except the sensation of being together. John felt an overwhelming sense of belonging with this woman, as though they were meant to be like this forever.

It couldn't last. He made sure she had her orgasm and after she'd came and he started to pull out, she stopped him. "Inside me."

"You sure?"

"Definitely. Go ahead. I can do another."

To their mutual thrill and amazement, she was right. They came at nearly the same time and were soon panting beside one another. John reached over for Katie's hand and she gave him a quick squeeze.

"Damn." She gasped. "I don't want you to time jump again, but if you do, I guess there's an upside."

They shared a giggle before getting up to shower.

Chapter 10

All Good Things

Dungallow, Scotland
December 31, 2019

"Hurry up, hon! I don't want to miss a minute of my New Year's with my guy." Katie was standing at the top of the stairs leading down to the basement.

"Be right up!" John hollered back. They'd been working on making the basement serve a few purposes, as a more private place for John to work in with a photography dark room and a small study. He put aside his hammer and wiped his forehead with a handkerchief. It wouldn't be long before New Years, and here he was building away.

John decided to grab a quick shower and then head back downstairs to spend the last few hours of the evening with Katie. It would just be the two of them this time, they'd agreed; friends and family might be part of the next New Year's Eve celebrations. 2020 was meant to be just for them.

When he'd hopped in the shower and felt the warm water washing away the sweat of a day's work, he heard the door open. From the shadow outside of the shower, he saw Katie's clothes falling away.

"Are we celebrating a little early?"

She stepped in and they embraced, kissing. "I have something to share with you and, well, I can't think of a more intimate place to tell you." Her voice was cracking as she spoke and she looked like she was about to cry.

John reached across and touched her cheek gently. "Oh, hon. Don't be sad. Whatever it is, I think we can work it out. I'm here for you, I promise."

She sniffed and smiled. "I'm not sad, but you'd better be here for us. We're counting on you."

He nodded. "Of course. Whatever you- wait. We?"

"Now he gets it." She laughed and searched his eyes for a response.

For a moment he was speechless. Then he shouted with unrestrained glee, "Seriously? Seriously, wow! I can't believe it!"

"Don't jump up and down hon. It's a small shower!" She teased. She was about to say something more, but he stopped her with a deep, lingering kiss.

***

The couple were sitting in front of the television, each holding a cup of eggnog. John had bought champagne for the occasion earlier in the week, but in light of the newest revelation, he'd agreed to forego it.

"That ball is never going to drop." He laughed. "And the musical act is just terrible."

It was already the New Year in Scotland, but the couple had agreed to stay up into the wee hours and watch the ball drop in America. They were British in spirit, but there would always be an element of their homeland in them.

"I kind of like them." Katie shrugged. They looked at each other and shared a laugh.

"I refuse to argue music with you, on today of all days. Or about anything else. In fact, I promise not to argue with you at all for the rest of the year."

She scoffed. "There's only five minutes left of 2019. American 2019, anyway. Big promise."

"Hey, I bet I can do it."

"Bet you can't." Katie countered

"Yes I can!" She raised an eyebrow and he snapped his fingers. "You win, as always."

Katie leaned back in the crook of his arm. "I know what I want to name her. Or him."

"Oh? Do I get a say?"

She looked up innocently. "Middle name?"

He chuckled. "I guess. But if I hate the names you pick, I'm going to say so. It's only fair."

She nodded. "If she's a girl, I'd like to name her Lair. In memory of my daughter." Lair had been her child in Roman-era Britain, born before her counterpart had met and partnered with John's counterpart. He quickly agreed to the name. Lair had been special to them both.

"And if it's a boy?" He asked. He thought he knew what the answer would be, but he was okay with it.

"Diarmad. For... for him." He knew she was referring to her long-dead husband in medieval Scotland. It was behind them and no longer an issue. Her past was her past.

"Well, the middle names would have to be Iona and Malcolm. If you're fine with that." He gently ran his hand through her long hair, playing with the tresses.

"More than fine." She pointed to the TV. "Ooh, check it out. The countdown is starting."

They watched as the ball, far away back in their home country, prepared for its long descent. 2020 was nearly upon them in their adopted country.

"There it goes." They shared a quiet, slow kiss, holding each other and happy in one another's arms. When they parted, Katie said something he didn't catch.

~ One Last Time ~

"Say that again, love?" He asked and she leaned in to whisper in his ear.

"I'm yours and you're mine for all the rest of time."

***

Preview of the next book in the series...

"Into The Rennaisance"

~ One Last Time ~

Chapter 1

The Cruise Home

The Atlantic Ocean

May 10, 2031

Gazing at the northern ocean from the starboard side of the *Ocean Vanguard* were a family trio of figures of alternating height. They were alone on the deck at this hour, long past the bedtime of the shortest of the three. But they didn't mind the lonely nature of their vigil. They were busy stargazing.

"What's that shape, sweet pea?" Asked the tallest of the family, a man wearing a flat, brown driver's cap. He was cupping his chin, stroking the brown beard that had recently begun to develop many flecks of white and grey. John could dye his hair as his wife had taken to doing, but he preferred to go naturally grey.

"Pa! Don't call me that."

"Oh no! I can't call you sweet pea?" He sounded hurt, but winked at his wife, Katie. She smirked in response.

"That's a baby name. I'm nine now." The slight, ginger-haired girl protested. But even as she complained, she was giggling a little. This wasn't a new game between them.

"What should I call you, then? Gum drop? Princess Buttercup?"

"Lair, please, Pa."

"Oh. Well, little Lair Duncan, which constellation am I pointing to?"

She squinted at the night sky. "That looks like Orion the Hunter to me."

"No, my sweet. He's not visible in the evening, remember? He's in our northern skies during the day."

"Oh." She looked annoyed and stamped her feet. "I'm cold. Can we go back inside?"

"All right. We'll continue this lesson tomorrow and try again, shall we?"

She nodded enthusiastically, and John swept her up off the deck and into his arms. The little girl leaned her head against his shoulder, and started sucking her thumb. He gently but firmly touched her hand as a reminder and she removed it from her mouth.

"I forgot."

Katie spoke up after brushing the girl's hair out of her face. "Try to remember, sweetie. It's a bad habit."

"I know! I'm sorry."

"It's okay." The Duncans stepped into the warm embrace of a stairway entry leading up to their suite.

On land, John and Katie didn't attempt to live ostentatiously. They kept a modest rural home in the little village of Dungallow, Scotland, and they owned small apartments in London and Glasgow for frequent visits with friends and for work-related trips. With their millions, they could have easily kept up multiple homes and invested heavily in real estate. John had even suggested they buy a castle when it went on the market, and she had persuaded him to pass. However, at sea it was a different story.

They hadn't taken a cruise since their world tour just before Lair was born. It had quickly become apparent to them that for extremely long voyages such as this transatlantic crossing, comfort was well worth the investment. For Lair, it was something of a wonderland. They'd taken a grand duplex suite with two bathrooms, one just for Lair. Though it featured only one bed, they'd had the desk nook in the lower portion of the suite removed for a guest bed instead. With a kitchen, dining area, online nook, treadmill, and private deck, their little living area was one of the nicest spaces onboard the ship.

"How long until we're in America?" She asked her parents sleepily as they found the door to their suite. Other couples, mostly in their 60's or older, were returning to their own suites dressed in tuxedos and elegant dresses. There had been a ballroom dance of some sort, it appeared, just as there had been the past few days of the cruise.

"I told you, three more days." Katie reminded her. She went ahead of the pair and turned down the Lair's bed sheets.

"That seems long." John lingered in the kitchen with their daughter, fetching her a drink of milk first. Good planning, Katie thought. She was bound to ask.

John and Lair appeared with the milk and he set his daughter into bed. "Read me a story." She asked, taking the cup with both hands and gulping.

~ One Last Time ~

"Go slow, love." John suggested. He sat beside her on the bed and Katie decided to leave them to it. She'd do reading duties tomorrow, anyway. Instead, she went to the neighboring living room and lay back on the couch, listening in.

"Tell me about when you and Ma stopped the Romans." She heard Lair and John shifting on the bed, each trying to get comfortable for the tale.

"Oh, you've heard all that time-traveling stuff before. It's old, you know. Why not a lovely story about the swans of Ireland, or perhaps the shoemaker's elves?"

"No, I want to hear about the girl I was named for. Ma's other daughter."

John sighed. "Well, you know she's long dead. We traveled back in time, as I said, and it was there that we were thought to be other people."

"Your ancestors?" Lair interrupted.

"Yes, that's what we think. Your Ma had a daughter by the name of Lair, and she fell in love with a Roman artist. They painted our pictures in the caves I took you to last summer, do you remember?"

"I do!" She exclaimed. John proceeded to tell her of their adventures as Pict warriors, leaving out the gorier aspects of the tale.

"That's how you came to be named Lair." He concluded. "We stopped the Romans and they didn't invade the little Pict village. But we travelled many other times to other centuries. Though some people don't believe us, your Ma and I are certain of what happened. We lived it, you see."

"Malcolm Stuart doesn't believe it. He told me so in school." She sounded irritated.

"As I said, there are those who can't accept what we've told them. It's their problem, not ours. Anything else before bed?"

"No. I can't wait to see America! New York and Chicago must be so exciting."

"They are. You want to know what they have that's really exciting?"

"What?"

"Self-driving cars. They're becoming very common in the big cities, I'm told."

She scoffed at this. "Yeah, they have those in London. Ma showed me when we went there for her book signing."

"I forget you're so worldly. Much more than I think. Good night sweet pea."

This time she didn't object. "Night Pa."

John returned to the living room and sat down on the couch beside Katie. Katie lifted her legs and rested them on his lap, and he began to massage them. "She's getting harder to get to sleep."

"I know. All she wants to do is hear you tell stories." Katie yawned and stretched. "That feels nice. Do my feet too."

"Head upstairs with me and you'll get the full body treatment." He suggested.

She scoffed. "That sounds like you have other expectations, Mr. Duncan."

"No more than that of an innocent masseuse, Madame, plying his trade. Of course, I do offer the bonus service for the more discerning client."

They got up and started up the stairs. "I don't tip." She teased, holding his hand and leading the way.

"We'll call this one gratis, madame."

"Hmm. We'll see." They slipped into their dark stateroom and Katie gazed out at the vast Atlantic ocean behind them, leaving a watery roadway back to Europe and home.

***

~ One Last Time ~

Grab your copy of

"Into The Rennaisance"

Available on Amazon or at a store near you. Liked what you've read? Check out other books available from SubArctic Publishing on Amazon.

About the Author

From Scotland to Egypt, South America to Japan - travel the world in romance. William Newell enjoys creating imaginative novellas which are captivating. Come home each evening and explore a deep relationship between animated characters while learning the history of a new part of the world.

William is passionate about creating deep connections between the characters in his works to bring them alive off the page, while adding a modern twist to their everyday obstacles. Expect humor and whit while living the adventure in the richly detailed canvas of these stories.

His goal is to enrich and entertain, providing an avenue of enjoyment which sparks the creativity and imagination of his readers. Besides writing, William's passion is learning about the history of the world's most unique cultures. He aims to weave his own knowledge into each individual story he creates.

Visit William Newell's Author Page on Amazon.

Manufactured by Amazon.ca
Bolton, ON

30058084R00069